Just in Rhyme

IN THE GARDEN

by Toni McKay-Lawton

Illustrated by Eddie Manning

Ransom

butterflies are full of grace
with pretty dainty wings
what makes them even
                        better though
is that they have no stings

caterpillars are short and fat
and really very wobbly
they come in many shapes
you see
sometimes they're even bobbly

spiders are a naughty bunch
with legs all long and hairy
they like to settle in the bath
hoping to look big and scary

a ladybird is round and cute
with spots upon its back
they're really very nice and small
and come in red and black

wasps are yellow and black you know
some have a silly grin
they like to buzz round sticky stuff
but watch out for their sting